IN THE
LAND OF WORDS

NEW AND SELECTED POEMS

BY ELOISE GREENFIELD

ILLUSTRATED BY JAN SPIVEY GILCHRIST

HarperCollins*Publishers*

 Amistad

ACKNOWLEDGMENTS

Thanks to Antoinette Fogg
Special thanks to my cousin,
Jerlean McAlister, for that
extra hand when I needed it.
Love you
—J.S.G.

In the Land of Words: New and Selected Poems
Compilation copyright © 2004 by Eloise Greenfield
Illustrations copyright © 2004 by Jan Spivey Gilchrist
Printed in the U.S.A. All rights reserved.
www.harperchildrens.com

Library of Congress Cataloging-in-Publication Data
Greenfield, Eloise.
In the land of words : new and selected poems / by Eloise Greenfield ; illustrated by Jan Spivey Gilchrist.
p.   cm.
Includes index.
ISBN 0-06-028993-7 — ISBN 0-06-028994-5 (lib.)
1. Children's poetry, American.   [1. American poetry.]   1. Gilchrist, Jan Spivey, ill.   II. Title.
PS3557.R39416 I5   2004
811'.54—dc21   2001024599
Typography by Stephanie Bart-Horvath
1 2 3 4 5 6 7 8 9 10
❖
First Edition

To Judy Richardson
for the skill and integrity she brings
to her work as a documentarian
and for her friendship
—E.G.

For my sisters, Sular, Mary, Gail, Mable, and Ina,
and in loving memory of Vicki and Melba
—J.S.G.

ALSO BY ELOISE GREENFIELD

Africa Dream, illustrated by Carole Byard

Childtimes: A Three-Generation Memoir,
with Lessie Jones Little and illustrated by Jerry Pinkney

For the Love of the Game: Michael Jordan and Me,
illustrated by Jan Spivey Gilchrist

Honey, I Love and Other Love Poems,
illustrated by Diane and Leo Dillon

Honey, I Love, illustrated by Jan Spivey Gilchrist

How They Got Over: African Americans and the Call of the Sea,
illustrated by Jan Spivey Gilchrist

I Can Draw a Weeposaur and Other Dinosaurs,
illustrated by Jan Spivey Gilchrist

Mary McLeod Bethune, illustrated by Jerry Pinkney

Me and Neesie, illustrated by Jan Spivey Gilchrist

Rosa Parks, illustrated by Gil Ashby

She Come Bringing Me That Little Baby Girl,
illustrated by John Steptoe

Sister, illustrated by Moneta Barnett

Talk About a Family, illustrated by James Calvin

Under the Sunday Tree, illustrated by Amos Ferguson

Water Water, illustrated by Jan Spivey Gilchrist

William and the Good Old Days,
illustrated by Jan Spivey Gilchrist

AUTHOR'S NOTE

I am often asked by children where my words—the words that I shape into stories and poems—come from. I don't always know the answer.

The words can come from a memory, or a dream, or something I see or hear or wonder about or imagine. But sometimes they just flow into my head and surprise me, and I have no idea how they got there.

Maybe there's a place where words live, where our minds and hearts can go and find them when we want to write—or read.

I like to imagine that there *is* such a place. I call it "The Land of Words."

Won't you come with me now for a visit to this land?

Eloise Greenfield

CONTENTS

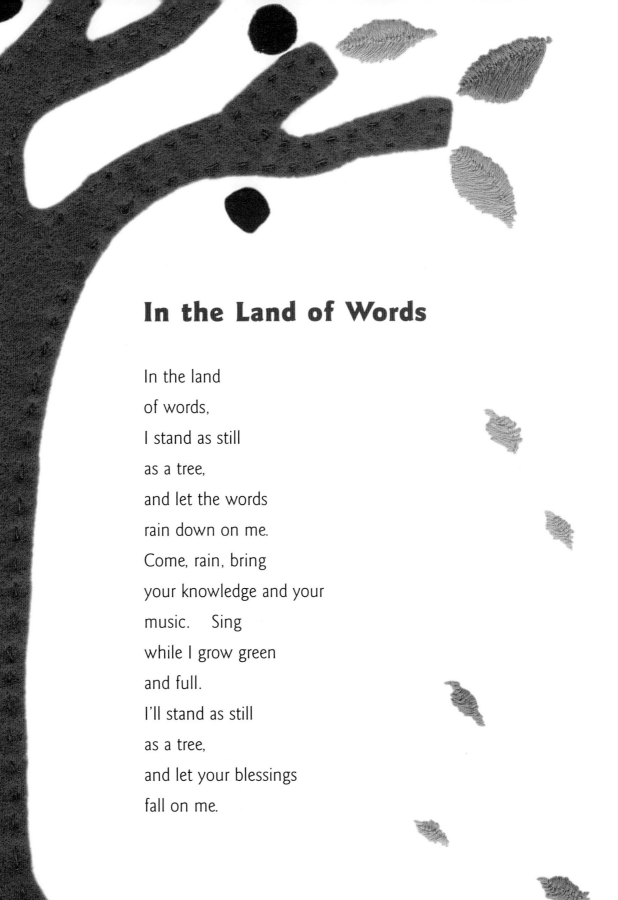

In the Land of Words

In the land
of words,
I stand as still
as a tree,
and let the words
rain down on me.
Come, rain, bring
your knowledge and your
music.   Sing
while I grow green
and full.
I'll stand as still
as a tree,
and let your blessings
fall on me.

Part I

The Poet/
The Poem

Nathaniel's Rap

Many children believe that my Nathaniel is real, and he is real—but only in the world of my imagination. I don't know how or why he came to me, but I kept going into that world to see him. I watched him live, I heard him speak. I know him well. I love him.

It's Nathaniel talking
and Nathaniel's me
I'm talking about
my philosophy
About the things I do
And the people I see
All told in the words
Of Nathaniel B. Free
That's me
And I can rap
I can rap
I can

rap,
rap,

rap   Till your earflaps flap

I can talk that talk
Till you go for a walk
I can run it on down
Till you get out of town

I can rap

I can rap

Rested, dressed and feeling fine
I've got something on my mind
Friends and kin and neighborhood
Listen now and listen good
Nathaniel's talking
Nathaniel B. Free
Talking about
My philosophy

Been thinking all day
I got a lot to say
Gotta run it on down
Nathaniel's way
Okay!
I gotta rap
Gotta rap
Gotta rap, rap, rap
Till your earflaps flap
Gotta talk that talk
Till you go for a walk
Gotta run it on down
Till you get out of town

Gotta rap

Gotta rap

Rested, dressed and feeling fine
I've got something on my mind
Friends and kin and neighborhood
Listen now and listen good

I'm gonna rap, hey!
Gonna rap, hey!
Gonna rap, hey!

I'm gonna rap!

To Catch a Fish

This poem was inspired by a painting by Amos Ferguson.
I thought of the patience it takes to go fishing.

It takes more than a wish
to catch a fish
you take the hook
you add the bait
you concentrate
and then you wait
you wait   you wait
but not a bite
the fish don't have
an appetite
so tell them what
good bait you've got
and how your bait
can hit the spot
this works a whole
lot better than
a wish
if you really
want to catch
a fish

Keepsake

When I was a small child, one of my neighbors, a very kind man, died. His wife gave me a penny when she saw how sad I was. She said it was a gift from him, but I think now that it may have been a gift from her, that she put her own sadness aside for a moment to try to comfort a child. In writing the poem, I changed the details but tried to capture the feeling.

Before Mrs. Williams died

She told Mr. Williams

When he gets home

To get a nickel out of her

Navy blue pocketbook

And give it to her

Sweet little gingerbread girl

That's me

I ain't **never** going to spend it

New Baby Poem (I)

*I was thinking about how a new little baby
might feel in a big crib, a big room, a big world.*

all day she has slept
now is her time
to cry
"Where am I?
I'm too tiny a girl
for this big new world."

New Baby Poem (II)

*What do babies dream about?
They can't tell us. I tried to guess.*

sleep coming down
bringing dreams that
swish
like the sound of
warm water
rocking the baby
rocking the baby
Swish, swish,
swish.

Way Down in the Music

I love music. There are times when I feel as if I'm down inside the music, it's swirling over my head and all around me, and nothing exists in the whole world, except the music and me.

I get way down in the music
Down inside the music
I let it wake me
      take me
Spin me around and make me
Uh-get down

20

Inside the sound of the Jackson Five
Into the tune of Earth, Wind and Fire
Down in the bass where the beat comes from
Down in the horn and down in the drum
I get down
I get down

I get way down in the music
Down inside the music
I let it wake me
        take me
Spin me around and shake me
I get down, down
I get down

Making Friends

When my son was in kindergarten, he was fascinated that one of his class-mates could imitate a rabbit. She'd make long ears by sticking her fingers up on her head, she'd shape her mouth like a rabbit's, and top it all off by wiggling her nose.

when I was in kindergarten
this new girl came in our class one day
and the teacher told her to sit beside me
and I didn't know what to say
so I wiggled my nose and made my bunny face
and she laughed
then she puffed out her cheeks
and she made a funny face
and I laughed
so then
we were friends

Flowers

Jan Spivey Gilchrist sent me a drawing she had done of her husband and her daughter. She asked if I would write a poem about stepfathers. As I looked at the drawing, I could see and feel the love and care of a father, and the words came.

My stepfather brought me flowers today.
For my first solo—my first bouquet,

yellow **and** peach
and purple and red,

"Daughter, you sang like an angel," he said.
My stepfather brought me flowers, and I
pretended there wasn't a tear in his eye,
flowers and happiness tied with a bow,
because I had just sung my first solo.

Excerpt from
Family

These are childhood memories. When I began writing them, I used many words and I punctuated them in the usual way. But the memories didn't run one into the other the way memories often do in our thoughts. I kept going back to the page, crossing out words, and more words, and periods and commas, until I found the feeling I wanted.

Saturday Sunday mornings
Daddy making pancakes
big as the plate Daddy
making fat hamburgers

leftover stuffed with rice
green peas enough for
everybody. . . . Lincoln Park
evenings Mama other mothers
bench-talk children playing. . . .
Downtown Wilbur Gerald Eloise
wait in the car have fun get
mad have fun get mad. . . . Vedie
little sister turning somersaults
we laugh. Vera baby sister
sweet baby laughing we laugh. . . .

Parade take turns on Daddy's

shoulder watch the floats

watch the firemen march

watch the horns watch

the sound of the bass

drum. . . . Easter Monday picnic

zoo dyed eggs lionhouse

popcorn polar bear picnic.

Merry-go-round Mama laughing.

Sparrow's Beach sun

water-splashing sandy legs

Mama laughing.

mama laughing. . . .

Family.

Part II

In the Land

Books

I've got
Books on the bunk bed
Books on the chair
Books on the couch
And every old where

But I want more books
I just can't get enough
I want more books about
All kinds of stuff, like
      Jackie's troubles
      Raymond's joys
      Rabbits, kangaroos
      Girls and boys
      Mountains, valleys
      Winter, spring
      Campfires, vampires
      Every old thing

I want to

Lie down on my bunk bed

Lean back in my chair

Curl up on the couch

And every old where

And

read

more

books!

Story

I step into the story,
I leave my world behind,
I let the walls of story
Be the walls around my mind.

New faces and new voices,
I listen and I see,
and people I have never met
mean everything to me.

I worry when they worry,
I quake when danger's near,
I hold my breath and hope
that all their troubles disappear.

I don't know what will happen,
I never know what I'll find,
when I step into a story
and leave my world behind.

Twister

He can't say it,
she can't say it.
Can I say it? No.

We have to say it
fast, of course,
no fair to say it slow.
It twists our tongues,
it twists our brains,
our faces start to frown.
But I bet it would be
a bit better, buddies—
if we could slow it down.
Come on, let's slow it down.

Jokes

Every day we get together
to see who can tell
the funniest joke.
We don't even have to vote.
It's always Crystal
who wins.
The words come flying
out of her mouth,
straight to the center
of our funny bones,
tickling us into
losing the game
and loving it.

Riddles

The ones I like the most
are the ones that make you
think and think,
while everybody waits,
hoping you'll give up.
Give up? Not me.
I'll get it.
You'll see.

Poet/Poem

Poet: Where are you, words,
        the ones that will fit
        the thoughts I am thinking,
        as here I sit?

Poem: Hiding, I'm hiding,
       I let you see
       only the smallest
       part of me.
       If you want to see more,
       you'll have to go deep
       into the forest
       where I sleep.

Poet: But suppose I get lost?
Poem: You might.
Poet: I'm afraid.
Poem: All right. Good-bye.
Poet: Wait! Don't go.
       I'll try.

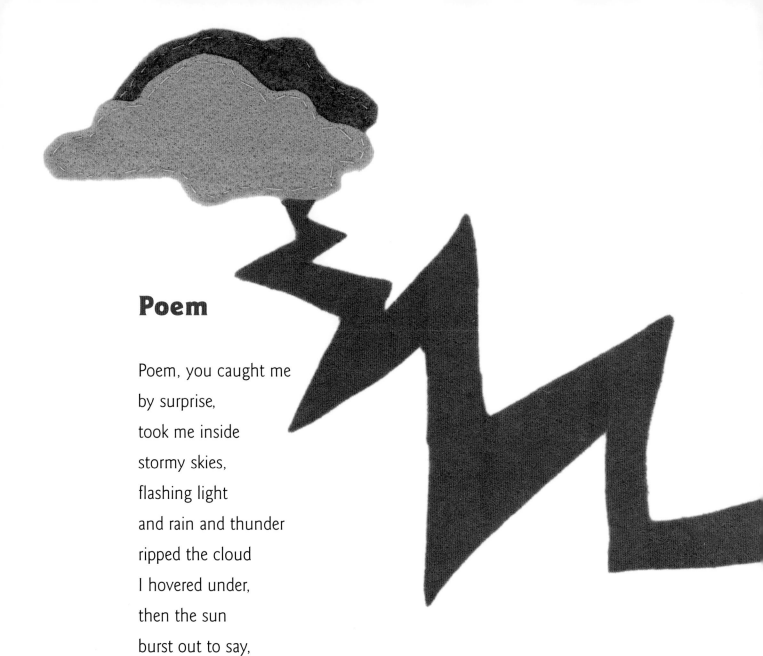

Poem

Poem, you caught me
by surprise,
took me inside
stormy skies,
flashing light
and rain and thunder
ripped the cloud
I hovered under,
then the sun
burst out to say,
"Get back, storm,
you're in my way!"
What a brightness,
what a glow,
thank you, Poem,
for such a show,
and when I am
back at home,
I won't forget you,
Poem.

Two Poems

The first one made me
smile a bit,
laugh out loud
at the end of it.

The next one almost
made me cry.
Did the butterfly
have to die?

Two poems entered
magically,
and touched two places
inside of me.

Oh, Words

Oh, I love those wacky words,
those crazy words that crack me up,
like *dibbily-doobily-doo* and such,
they don't mean much,
but oh, I love them so.

Oh, I love those wicked words,
those mean, mean words
from the mouths of sorcerers,
who point and yell
and cast a spell, saying,
"You will sleep for a thousand
years,
I will not change,
so stop your tears. *Sleep!"*
And the good folks fall
and then lie still,
while I hug myself
to hold the chill
brought on by those
wicked words.

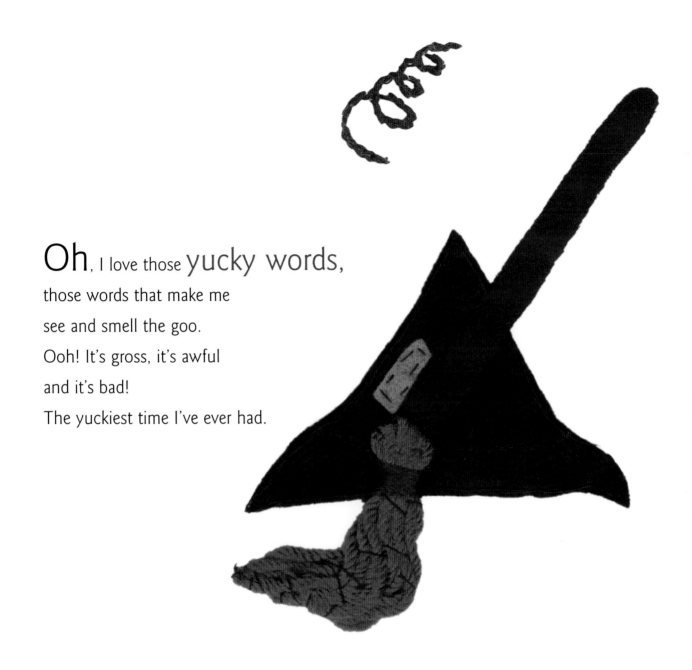

Oh, I love those yucky words,
those words that make me
see and smell the goo.
Ooh! It's gross, it's awful
and it's bad!
The yuckiest time I've ever had.

Words, oh, words,
Oh, what a mess,
Wicked, wacky, yucky,
Yes!

I Don't Care

When I go shopping with my big brother,
He tries on one shirt after another,
But I don't ever really care,
As long as I have a book and a chair.

On a family ride that's many miles long,
I don't sing that boredom song,
I never say, "Are we almost there?"
I have my book, and I don't care.

A minute ago, Mama tried to tease,
"John, come look! A dancing cheese!"
I didn't laugh, I didn't look,
My head is buried in my book.

Later, I'll think of a cheese with eyes,
Nose and mouth and legs and thighs,
A cheese that tangos down the stair,
But right now, I just don't care!

I Go to the Land

I go to the land of words,
for I am at home there,
and never leave
for long. My thirst
pushes me through
the open door.
The more I drink
of the falling water,
the more I know.
I drink. I think.
I grow.

SOURCES

"Books" from Children's Book Council bookmark. Copyright © 1979 by Eloise Greenfield.

Excerpt from "Family" from *Childtimes: A Three-Generation Memoir* (HarperCollins [originally T. Y. Crowell]). Copyright © 1979 by Eloise Greenfield and Lessie Jones Little.

"Flowers" from *Angels* (Hyperion Books for Children). Copyright © 1999 by Eloise Greenfield.

"In the Land of Words" from Coretta Scott King Award thirtieth anniversary poster (Hyperion Books for Children). Copyright © 1999 by Eloise Greenfield.

"Keepsake" and "Way Down in the Music" from *Honey, I Love* (HarperCollins [originally T. Y. Crowell]). Copyright © 1978 by Eloise Greenfield.

"Making Friends" and "Nathaniel's Rap" from *Nathaniel Talking* (Black Butterfly Children's Books). Copyright © 1988 by Eloise Greenfield.

"New Baby (I)" and "New Baby (II)" from *Night on Neighborhood Street* (Dial Books for Young Readers). Copyright © 1991 by Eloise Greenfield.

"Poem" from Children's Book Council bookmark. Copyright © 1999 by Eloise Greenfield.

"To Catch a Fish" from *Under the Sunday Tree* (HarperCollins). Copyright © 1988 by Eloise Greenfield.

INDEX